Yankee Doodle on the FRONTiER

Al Hartley

MULTNOMAH

Here it is, folks . . .
the 1800 model
family convertible!

Not much horsepower,
but still, lots of get up and go!

Loads of trunk space . . .
room for the whole family, their
tools, and their dreams!

I led thousands of these
wagons,[1] into the old frontier!

Believe me, these models never
burned rubber at a traffic light! Speed
was measured in *feet*,[2] not *miles* per hour!

They groaned and creaked up
and down mountains. The cow's milk sort of
churned itself as it bounced along.

And young ones had so much fun along the trail,
they never asked, "When do we get there?"

When they came to a river,
the wagons stopped *creaking* and started
leaking![3]

If they didn't leak too badly,
there was time to do the wash
and try fishing.

But these folks weren't on a picnic.
The hills ahead were full of surprises!

When a good piece of land was found,
the pioneers became
the frontier's first do-it-yourselfers!

They cut *down* trees
and then cut them *up*!

They knew a strong,
safe home was job one!

The neighbors watched
but didn't like what was
happening to the neighborhood.

They decided to throw a party!
But they weren't thinking
fun and games!

How's this for the
local welcome wagon?

The new home became
a fortress in a hurry!

The pioneers seemed safe inside,
but their livestock sure weren't.

And, of course, the more that was
stolen, the less folks had to eat.

Talk about a *house warming*!

This is how they did it
on the frontier.

And this wasn't action
on your friendly TV screen.

It was *live*!
It was going on
all around the house.
It certainly heated things up.

I saw an ugly mood
gallop across the frontier.

Folks were trying
to get even, and when
you start down that trail,
you never know where
it will end.

There were scoundrels
ready to break every law
of man and God!

Fur trappers[4], for example,
were jealous of "their" territory
and ready to catch
more than animals!

I felt this was God's country and there was plenty of room for folks to live together in peace . . . if there was enough room in their hearts!

A tug-of-war was going on.
Right and wrong were choosing up
sides, and wrong was winning!

I saw things
churning
like wash
at today's
laundromats.
It seemed to me
the frontier was
about to go
down the drain!

And yet, while the frontier was bringing out the *worst*, it also brought out the *best*!

The spirit of love came to the rescue of many in need.

In the meantime,
folks still poured
into the frontier.

They built forts for protection
when danger came!

And into the
tug-of-war
rode another force!

The circuit rider![5]
He rode trails called circuits!
And he brought what was badly
needed . . . a road map that led out
of all the fighting and fear
on the frontier. He brought the Bible!

The circuit rider brought
wisdom that the youngest
pioneer could understand:

Families and frontiers
can't hold together if
everyone goes their own way!

He spread the good news[6]
of a better way to go!

Soon folks were gathering
with banjos instead of rifles!

And wives brought high caliber
ammunition for a picnic!

We all agreed
banjos and fiddles
sounded better
than rifles!

And the ammunition really hit the spot.

But still, life on the frontier wasn't exactly a visit to Camp Whoopee!

We were living in a new, tough environment!

Weather could wipe out precious crops at any time!

PLANTING LIST

CORN
SQUASH
PUMPKINS
POTATOES
CABBAGE
CARROTS
BEANS

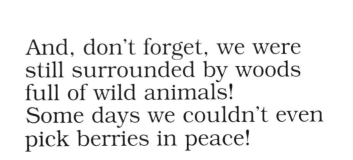

And, don't forget, we were
still surrounded by woods
full of wild animals!
Some days we couldn't even
pick berries in peace!

And yet, we needed the forest.
Its wood built our cabins
and heated them.

In fact,
we used wood
for everything
from the cradle
to the coffin!

Another thing . . . the forest was a supermarket of food and a giant medicine cabinet of roots and herbs[7] and leaves for all our aches and pains!

Do you love a parade?
How do you like this one?

These are your roots
spreading across America!

They came from different lands,
spoke different languages, but
they became one nation under God!
They *lived* the Pledge of Allegiance.[8]

Sure, pioneers have settled other lands. But America was a lot different! It was a whole new world with a new kind of freedom the old world had never seen before! Do you ever wonder why folks all over the world still want to live in America?

Our Pledge of Allegiance has the answer!
We're one nation under God!

It doesn't matter what color
we are or where we come from!

The big question is:
Where are we going?

We're all part of that great adventure of growth and freedom! In fact, the American adventure is more exciting than ever! Oh sure, things are different on the *outside* today . . . but they're still the same on the *inside*!

Naturally,
today's frontier
seems to be far away,
but our *personal* frontier[9]
is right *down to earth*.

And sometimes it seems
just as hard to keep our lives
safe down here as it is out there.

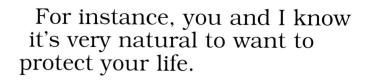

For instance, you and I know
it's very natural to want to
protect your life.

Especially if the danger is dressed
in war paint or has claws and sharp teeth!

But it's harder when the threat to your life is a wolf in sheep's clothing. It gets tricky when drugs that destroy us dress up as pleasant, exciting experiences, or seem to be symbols of being part of the gang![10]

So our big adventure today
isn't just *outer* space . . .
it's *inner* space.

It's the tug-of-war *inside* us!

The pull between what's *good*
for us and what's *bad* for us!

And to make the right choice!

The frontier grew up and became the greatest nation in history! You can grow up and have a special part in America's heritage!

Your Creator gave you special talents! Stand out! Be all you were meant to be!

And so, with that great adventure
ahead, we have one foot in the
old frontier and one in the new!

We have footsteps to follow,
and, thank God, we're free
to make our own!

May they be in *His* steps!

Notes

1. The pioneers used many types of wagons, some pulled by eight horses, some by oxen. Some were actually pulled by the pioneers themselves.
2. Some days the wagons traveled only one mile. The average distance per day was about twelve miles.
3. When there were several miles of river to travel, rafts were built to float the wagons.
4. Fur trappers usually preceded settlers into new territory.
5. There were two kinds of circuit riders--preachers and judges--both very important to life on the frontier. Abraham Lincoln rode a circuit for several years as a lawyer.
6. The "Good News" the circuit rider spread was the Gospel according to Matthew, Mark, Luke, and John.
7. In addition to treating illness, many plants, roots and leaves were used for such things as repelling insects, killing odors, etc.
8. I pledge allegiance to the flag of the United States of America, and to the republic for which it stands, one nation under God, indivisible, with liberty and justice for all.
9. Without a personal frontier and goal, life loses its adventure and purpose. No one is meant to be a mere spectator. The future is full of promise, but we must reach out for it.
10. Many of us know others who have made the mistake of trying something dangerous and destructive simply because a friend did it and thought it was fun.